THE DARK SIDE
of the CREEK

By Joan Hiatt Harlow
Illustrated by Fiona King

The Dark Side of the Creek
©2000 Wright Group Publishing, Inc.
By Joan Hiatt Harlow
Illustrated by Fiona King

SUNSHINE™
© Wright Group Publishing, Inc.

The Wright Group
19201 120th Avenue NE
Bothell, WA 98011
www.WrightGroup.com

Printed in Canada

10 9 8 7 6 5 4 3

ISBN: 0-322-01938-9
ISBN: 0-322-01941-9 (6-pack)

CONTENTS

CHAPTER 1
A Scream in the Night

I was in the middle of a really neat dream. I had just kicked the winning goal for my soccer team. Everyone was cheering for me. "Yay, Josh!"

Then their cheers turned into a horrible scream, and I woke up.

At first I didn't know where I was. Then I remembered. I was at my grandparents' house in Florida.

I had flown there from Oklahoma the day before. I had never traveled alone in a plane before that. It was kind of scary, but it was fun, too. Grandma and Grandpa met me when I got off the plane in Florida.

Now I was on winter vacation for two whole weeks. No mittens, no boots, no snow, and no homework! Best of all, I could go swimming and fishing.

I peeked out the open window by my bed. Trickle Creek glistened in the moonlight. A whippoorwill called. An owl hooted. Was the scream part of my dream?

Yeeooow!

Another screech cut through the night air. I dove under the blanket. That was no dream!

The scream was different from the howl of coyotes. I go camping a lot. I've heard coyotes calling to each other. This scream was shrill and frightful. And it was nearby!

Everything was quiet again, but I couldn't get back to sleep. I just lay there for a long time.

Slowly it began to get light, and I heard dishes rattling in the kitchen. I pulled on my bathing suit and tee shirt and headed for the kitchen.

Grandpa was at the sink, juicing oranges from the tree in the yard.

"Good morning, Josh. Going swimming,
I see." He poured me a glass of juice.

Grandma scrambled some eggs and
tossed them into a sizzling pan. "Be sure to
sign in at the office," she reminded me.

"Helps to keep things safe," Grandpa
added.

My grandparents live at a retirement
place. It has everything: swimming pool,
recreation hall, hiking trails, even exercise
rooms. And no strangers are allowed.

I sat at the table and sipped my juice. "I heard something weird last night," I told them. "A loud, scary scream."

Grandma gave Grandpa a look. Then she scooped the eggs onto a plate. "We've heard the screams, too. They come from the other side of the creek." She placed the dish in front of me.

"Do you know what it is, Grandpa?" I asked. We're Native Americans. My grandpa's family has lived in this area for a long time. But he didn't answer. I saw another look pass between him and Grandma. Then he just passed the toast and said, "Stay away from the dark side of the creek, Joshua."

"The dark side?" I asked.

Grandpa shrugged. "That's just what I call it. It's still wild over there. I don't want you there by yourself." Through the window, the creek sparkled like a silver ribbon as it rippled its way to the bay. On this side, grassy lawns sloped down to the water. There were houses and swings and picnic tables—a friendly place.

The other side of the creek was like a jungle. Thick bushes and tall trees blocked out the sky. Spanish moss hung from the branches like giant spider webs. I remembered the screams and felt goose bumps on my arms.

After breakfast Grandpa pulled his red bike from the shed. "You can use this while you're here, Josh." He brushed it off with a rag. "I heard your friend Timothy Taylor is down from New Hampshire."

Tim was my best Florida friend last year. I couldn't wait to see him. I stuffed my towel in the bike basket. "He's probably at the pool already."

"When you get back, bring Tim and we'll go fishing," Grandpa called as I pedaled away.

I was right. When I arrived at the pool, Tim was already there. I parked my bike.

"Hi, Tim!"

"Yo! Josh!" he said, slapping me a high-five. He had gotten really tall and skinny since last winter. We both dove into the water.

"Guess who's here on vacation. The Orange Blossom Club." Tim was talking about Cassandra Kelly, "Cassie," and the twins, Denise and Melissa Alexander. Last year they had started the Orange Blossom Club. They wanted to be detectives and solve a mystery. They even tried to get us to join. No way would we be part of their club. Lucky we didn't, too. They went looking for a mystery to solve and got in trouble for spying on people in the park.

Tim and I swam for a while, until I remembered I hadn't registered.

"I have to sign in at the office." I got out of the water and wrapped myself in the towel.

"I'll go with you," said Tim.

We walked up the cement path to the recreation hall and into the office. Tom Birch, the manager, was at the desk. "Welcome back, Josh." He grinned. "I'm registering you right now. Let's see. Joshua Jacy." He scribbled my name in a book and then looked up at me over his glasses. "How long are you staying?"

"Two weeks," I answered.

"Keep in mind that this is a retirement park. Older folks don't want noise or trouble."

"We won't bother anyone," Tim said.

"Those girls are back. They caused a lot of trouble last year. They frightened old Mrs. Samuel when they hid out in her yard and spied on her." Mr. Birch frowned. "She thought they were burglars."

"Mr. Birch," I said, "I heard some screams coming from Trickle Creek last night. Do you know what could have made such terrible shrieks?"

Mr. Birch shook his head. "No, not me. Maybe you imagined it." Then he leaned over the counter. "You'd best stay away from there, if you know what's good for you," he warned.

CHAPTER 2
THE GECKOS

Mr. Birch took a deep breath and shook his head. "The man who owns that land doesn't want anyone trespassing. I'm warning you. He gets real mean when he's angry."

"Don't worry, Mr. Birch. We never cross the creek," said Tim.

"Besides," Mr. Birch continued, "there are snakes over there."

Tim and I headed for the door. That's when we saw the girls on the porch waving to us.

"Hi, guys," Cassie called. She looked older and even cuter this year.

Her red hair swung around her cheeks when she moved. "Want to join our club?" she asked.

"The Orange Blossoms?" Tim said with a snicker. "No, thanks."

Denise Alexander and her twin sister Melissa looked more alike than ever. They had dark eyes and their hair was as black as mine. Only mine is straight and always flopping into my eyes.

"We had to discontinue the Orange Blossoms," said Denise.

"We promised our folks," Melissa added.

"Now we're The Geckos," Cassie said.

"You mean like the chameleons?" Tim asked.

"No, Grandma says there are no chameleons in Florida," said Cassie. "Chameleons are from Africa." Cassie is real cute, but she's still a know-it-all.

"Then what do you call that?" Tim pointed to a tiny lizard scurrying across the porch railing.

"Actually, that's a green anole," Cassie said.

"It's also called a gecko," added Denise.

I was getting confused.

"They can slip into corners so they can't be seen," said Melissa.

"And they can climb anywhere, because they have little sticky pads on their feet," Denise continued.

"Isn't that a perfect name for a detective club?" asked Cassie. "The Geckos?"

"Besides, we decided 'Orange Blossoms' is kind of a dumb name," said Melissa.

Tim and I exchanged a look that said, *No kidding!*

"So, do you Geckos have a mystery to solve?" I asked.

"No," said Cassie. "Not yet."

"Josh does," Tim bragged. "A *real* mystery. He's heard blood-chilling screams from the other side of the creek. Tell them, Josh."

I began to think it might be fun to be a Gecko and solve the mystery. So I told them all about the screams. I made it sound like a horror story. All three girls listened with their eyes as big as pies. When I finished, Denise whispered, "That is so scary."

Melissa looked worried. "What's going on?"

But Cassie said, "Let's cross the creek and explore!"

I looked at her in astonishment. Either she was the bravest girl I've ever met or the craziest. "I'm not going to the dark side of the creek."

Tim nodded in agreement.

"Neither are we!" exclaimed Denise and Melissa together.

"Then how are we going to find out who was screaming?" Cassie asked. "Some detectives you are!"

"Right now I'm going fishing with my grandfather. Are you coming, Tim?" I asked.

As we hopped on our bikes, Cassie called, "The Geckos' first annual meeting will be held at the picnic shelter at noon. Bring your lunch."

Back at the house, Grandpa was waiting with the fishing poles, and Grandma had already fixed sandwiches.

"I talked with your grandparents, Tim," she said. "They know you're going fishing with Joshua and his grandpa."

Off we went—the three of us—to a bend in the creek where Grandpa said the fishing was good. The picnic shelter was just up the shore, so we'd see the girls when they showed up.

Grandpa nodded toward the other side of the creek. "Tom Birch says the retirement park wants to buy that land over there." He cast his fishing line into the water. "And there's another builder who'd like to construct a mall on the same spot. It would have to be changed to residential or business land. There's going to be a meeting at the town hall tomorrow night to discuss it. Most of us want the property to stay as is."

"Who owns the land?" I asked as I baited my hook.

"I don't know, but it's worth a lot of money." Something tugged at Grandpa's pole, and he began winding the reel. "Aw, it got away," he said.

Tim and I cast our lines. We sat on the bench and waited for a bite.

"All this land once belonged to Native Americans," said Grandpa.

"There are still some traces of early settlements in this area. There's a midden on the other side where the creek empties into the bay."

"What's a midden?" I jiggled my fishing pole a little.

"It's where our ancestors piled up seashells after they cleaned out the food." Grandpa stood up and cast his line again. "Yep. If someone buys that land another piece of native America will be gone forever."

"Can't they just leave the land like it is?" I asked.

"There is a group that might put up money to preserve the land. First, they'd need proof that the land is habitat for endangered birds or animals," Grandpa explained.

"Hey Josh! Tim!"

"The girls are waving at you from the picnic shelter," said Grandpa with a grin. "Better not keep them waiting."

"I'll leave my pole in the water," Tim said. "Maybe I'll catch something after all."

"Oh no," said Grandpa. "Pull it in. You shouldn't leave it unattended."

After we pulled in our lines, Grandpa gathered up the poles. Then Tim and I grabbed our lunch bags and raced to the picnic shelter to join the girls.

The round wooden shelter felt cool as we ate our lunches. Then Cassie stood up. "This is the first annual meeting of The Geckos. We must vote for officers."

"We don't need officers," I said.

Cassie ignored me. "We need someone to be president. Someone clever. Someone who is fearless and a born leader."

20

Tim looked around the picnic shelter. "And just who will that be?"

"Me, of course!" said Cassie.

"Oh, brother," I groaned.

That was when we heard terrible squawking from the creek. We jumped up and ran to the water's edge.

"Look!" Denise pointed to the other shore where a white bird was struggling to fly.

"That heron is all tangled up in fishing line," said Melissa.

"We've got to help him." Cassie had already kicked off her sandals and was wading out. The creek wasn't very deep because the tide was out.

"Watch out for alligators!" I yelled.

Cassie leaped back onto the shore and into her sandals.

"There's a log downstream that reaches the other side," said Tim. "Follow me."

We found the log and walked over it, one foot in front of the other, like tightrope walkers.

And there we were—on the dark side of the creek.

CHAPTER 3
Scary Discoveries

It wasn't easy untangling that heron. First we had to sneak up on the bird. The girls held their arms around him while Tim and I unraveled the fishing line.

Melissa screamed as the big bird wiggled and pecked. Tim and I slipped and sloshed around in the mud and even got tangled ourselves in the nylon line. When we finally set the bird free, we were covered in sand and mud and feathers.

"Someone got their fishing line snagged and just cut it and left it there," I said as I rolled up the line.

"I'll bet a lot of birds get hurt from fishing line," said Denise.

"That's why your grandpa said we should never leave a fishing pole unattended," Tim said.

Then Cassie pointed to the damp ground. "Hey, look at these huge tracks."

"Huge is right." I bent down to examine the large, flat footprints. "Whoever made them wasn't wearing ordinary shoes."

"You can hardly see the imprints of our sneakers," said Melissa. "But these tracks are so deep they look like tire treads. Somebody big made them."

"Look at the big letter Z in the middle of the sole," said Denise. "They're those expensive Zee brand of running shoes."

Cassie spoke up. "Let's see where they lead." She began pushing her way through the bushes.

At first no one moved. Then we all took off after her.

We followed a narrow footpath deeper into the woods. It's beautiful here, I thought, as bird songs mingled with the whisper of pine trees.

"Look! A zebra longwing!" Melissa pointed to a black-and-white striped butterfly that fluttered in the sunlight. "That's the official butterfly of Florida."

"Ouch! These plants have sharp edges," said Cassie as she led the way through the saw palmettos. She stopped in a clearing. "The footprints have disappeared."

"Look at this!" I pointed to a log on the side of the path that was covered with long scratches. It was scraped deeply, revealing the bare, white wood beneath the bark. "What could have made those claw marks?"

"Something with awfully long nails," said Denise. She clawed at the air with her bright red fingernails and made a scary face.

"That's not funny," Melissa scolded. "Whatever made those marks could be dangerous."

As we turned back, dark shadows flickered on the ground. I looked up. A flock of large, black birds circled above the trees. A few more hunched on branches.

"There's something dead nearby," I said.

Cassie turned pale. "Dead?"

Melissa and Denise grabbed each other. "Dead?"

"Those are vultures," I explained. "Grandpa says they're part of nature's clean-up patrol. They eat up all the roadkill and other dead things."

"Yuk!" Denise made a face.

"Well, someone's got to do it," said Tim with a smirk.

That's when I saw something under a tree. It looked like a pile of leaves and sticks,

but as I got closer I could see a hoof sticking out from beneath the rubble. I held my breath and lifted a few of the branches.

"What is it?" Tim asked. The girls were right behind him, peering over his shoulder.

I pulled the leaves back. What was left of an animal had been carefully covered.

"It's a wild hog!" Cassie exclaimed.

"It's half-eaten." I covered the carcass again. "No wonder the birds are circling."

"How did they see it?" Tim asked.

"Maybe they can smell anything that's dead," I answered.

Melissa shuddered. "Did you see the gashes on the back of its neck?"

Denise pulled on her sister's hand. "We're out of here! This place is creepy."

The twins bolted through the brush in the direction of the creek.

Cassie glanced fearfully toward the dead animal, and then raced after them. "Wait for me," she yelled.

Tim and I looked at each other. If Cassie was scared, we should be, too.

We flew after the girls, scratching our legs on the saw palmettos. When we reached the creek, we stopped in our tracks.

"The tide is coming in," Melissa groaned. "We can't get back!"

I had forgotten that the water in the creek changed with the tides. The log was a foot under water. The current looked swift, too.

Cassie looked around. "How can we get across?"

Just then a rowboat swung around the bend from upstream. A white-haired man was rowing.

"Are you kids stranded?" he called.

"Yes!" I answered. "We forgot about the tide."

Tim and I grabbed hold of the bow as the man pulled up to the shore. "Are you from the park?" We nodded. "Hop in and I'll take you back."

We scrambled into the boat gratefully, and in no time we were across the creek. The white-haired man steadied the boat as we climbed out. "What were you doing over there?"

"We went across to help a heron that was caught in fishing line," Cassie answered.

"It's beautiful there," I said.

The man nodded. "Yes, it is. I used to row up and down this creek when I was a boy. Many of the song birds I heard then have disappeared. I was listening today for the grasshopper sparrow. You have to listen carefully, because it's a weak song—like an insect or a cricket." He looked at us hopefully. "It likes the saw palmettos and dwarf oaks."

"We didn't hear it," said Denise.

"You probably wouldn't recognize it, anyway. It's an endangered bird now."

He pushed the boat out with his oar. "I was hoping..." The man sighed and didn't finish what he was about to say.

"Thanks for rescuing us," I called as I gave his boat a shove. "I hope you find your bird."

He nodded and waved.

"He is so nice," said Cassie.

Some of the park's residents were gathered under the shelter when we got back. Grandpa was standing in the middle of the group. "If we could prove the property is habitat for endangered animals or birds, the Society for the Protection of Land and Wildlife might purchase it," he was saying.

"The owner says there is no wildlife there that is endangered or threatened," said Mr. Taylor, Tim's grandpa.

Cassie's grandma spoke up. "Of course the owner would say that. He wants the money from the sale of the land."

"Well, he'd make a lot of money if it became a shopping mall," said another neighbor.

Mr. Alexander, the twins' grandpa sighed. "Seems like a hopeless cause."

"We can at least speak our mind at the meeting tomorrow," said Grandpa. "Maybe we can get people to vote against changing the property for business or residential use." Everyone nodded and walked away.

"Did you hear that?" I asked the other kids. "If we could prove there are endangered animals across the creek, we might save them—and save the land, too."

Denise shook her head. "You won't get me over there again."

"Not with dead things and mysterious screams," Melissa added.

"What about you, Tim?" I asked. "Should we go back and investigate?"

"I'm in," Tim answered quickly.

"I'm coming too," said Cassie.

"We'll go tomorrow at the first low tide," I said. "This time I'm bringing my camera."

"I'll bring my tape recorder," said Cassie, "in case we hear the grasshopper sparrow. Grandma says the scrub jay is a threatened bird, too."

"We've changed our minds," said Melissa.

Denise nodded. "After all, we're Geckos. We're coming too!"

CHAPTER 4
Danger!

I only half-slept that night. For one thing, I heard the screams again. What kind of animal could it be? I wondered. Then I thought about The Geckos exploring the dark side of the creek the next day. I couldn't get to sleep. I was too excited. I tossed and turned all night.

The morning news said the low tide would be around seven thirty. After breakfast I grabbed my camera and slung the strap around my neck. Then I headed to the shelter. Tim, Cassie, and the twins were already there.

"Good, you brought your camera. I have my tape recorder in here," said Cassie, patting her zippered pocket.

"Are we ready?" I asked.

"Let's go!" everyone answered.

The water in the stream was low as we crossed the slippery log to the dark side of the creek.

This time we found another narrow path that wound in an easterly direction.

"Wait," said Cassie. "I hear a bird." She pulled out her tape recorder. "I'm recording every bird song I hear. Who knows? One of them might be endangered."

While we waited for Cassie to record the song, I walked a little farther. "Look at this," I told Tim. In the soft damp earth were huge paw prints. "They're fresh!"

Tim pulled out his fishing tape and measured them. "About four inches wide! The animal must be heavy because the prints are deep."

"Four pads around a large central one. My German shepherd's tracks look something like that," said Cassie, "but my dog's tracks show claws. These don't."

"Whatever killed that hog had long, sharp claws," said Melissa.

We were all silent, trying to put the clues together.

Then I thought about my big cat, Morgan, back home. "Morgan uses his scratching post to sharpen his claws. Remember the claw marks on that log we saw yesterday? Maybe this is a cat and it's sharpening its claws, too!"

"It would have to be awfully big to make those marks," said Denise doubtfully.

"Besides, there are no claw marks in those tracks," added Melissa.

Cassie's face lit up. "Cats have claws, but they *retract!* They don't stick out all the time like a dog's claws."

"So cat tracks wouldn't show claw marks!" Tim exclaimed.

"Could it be a bobcat?" Cassie asked.

"The tracks are too big," I answered.

Denise looked scared. "A lion?"

"If a lion escaped from a zoo, we would have heard about it on the news," Melissa said.

"I know what it is!" I could hardly speak I was so excited. "And it *is* endangered."

"Tell us!" everyone said at once.

"The Florida panther!"

"Awesome!" Cassie's eyes were wide.

"No, I doubt it's a panther," said Denise. "They're rare and so timid."

"It's *got* to be the panther," Tim argued. "I've read that panthers kill hogs and deer, and cover the meat in a—a cache! Just like the dead thing we found yesterday."

"If we can prove it, maybe people will vote against selling the land for development," I said.

"And the panther can keep its home," added Melissa.

Cassie had her hands on her knees examining the tracks. She gasped, "There are those Zee-brand shoe prints again. Someone is tracking the panther. Let's follow them!"

As we moved along, the ground became hard and dry and both sets of prints faded.

"Now what?" Tim asked.

"Shhh! I hear a chirping. Maybe it's one of those rare sparrows." We all got quiet. Cassie turned on her tape recorder.

Then we heard another noise. Human voices!

"Come on," I whispered. Quietly and cautiously we crept closer to the sounds. Then, as the narrow path turned, it suddenly opened into a grove of pine trees. Two men were right in front of us, talking.

We ducked behind the saw palmettos and huddled low to the ground, afraid to move.

"What's taking you so long? I'm paying you a lot of money to get this job done," yelled the tall blond man.

"Panthers are clever. It's not easy to find them," the second man responded. He was so close, I could just see his black-and-white running shoes with a *Z* on the sides. Then he turned, and I saw the rifle cradled in his arms!

I had an idea. I lifted my camera between the palmetto branches and aimed it. I concentrated on stilling my shaking hands.

Click! The sound was muffled by the men's angry voices.

"We both know there's a family of panthers on this property. You'd better remove them before someone finds out. There's big money here, and I don't intend to lose it!" the blond man yelled again. "Those conservationists will raise a ruckus to save the panthers' habitat. Then the developers may back off. People who don't want to see the land changed have already organized a big town meeting tonight."

Suddenly I recalled Tom Birch's words. *The man who owns the land can get real mean when he's angry.* He was right.

"I have someone who wants the animals for his private zoo," the hunter growled. "He's willing to pay a lot. But I've got to find them, tranquilize them with this dart gun, and get them into a truck, all by myself. It's not easy."

"You've got until tomorrow!" I didn't like the way the man's mouth twisted when he spoke. He headed for a path away from us, then swung around and shouted, "Otherwise the deal is off, and I'll find someone else." He disappeared into the woods.

The hunter muttered something, and then checked his dart gun and walked off in the opposite direction.

"Let's get out of here!" I whispered.

We dashed back to the creek, crossed the log, and sank onto the benches of the picnic shelter.

Cassie held up her tape recorder. "I think the folks at the town meeting will be interested in this!" she said. "I got every word!"

CHAPTER 5
Geckos to the Rescue!

When I got back, I told Grandpa and Grandma about The Geckos and our discovery.

"We should have realized those were panther screams." Grandma smiled. "Did you know panthers purr, just like your cat Morgan?"

"That hunter was going to sell those animals for illegal trade," Grandpa said. He was furious. He pulled out his car keys. "Give me your film, Joshua. I can get it developed in an hour. I have a plan for the meeting tonight." I handed him the camera.

That evening Grandpa and all of us Geckos found seats up front. By seven o'clock the hall was full.

"Looks like just about everyone in town cares about the future of that land," Mr. Taylor said.

Four people sat in a line in the front of the room, facing the rest of us. The town manager went to the microphone. "Well, you all know why we're here," he said, "so we'd better get right to it. As our first speaker, let me introduce Charles Leon."

Cassie nudged me. It was the blond man we'd seen in the woods.

He started talking about how the land had belonged to his family for generations. He said it should be developed for taxes that would be used for the good of the town.

Then, Tom Birch showed a map of the property as a retirement park. There would be five hundred house lots, a golf course, and two more swimming pools. He grinned. "Once you folks vote to make this *residential* property, the park will make an offer to buy it."

Next, a real estate woman spoke. "If we build a shopping mall, there will be restaurants, supermarkets, department stores—everything you folks need. Once you make the change to *business* land, we'll purchase the property and start clearing it."

Next, the president of the Society for the Protection of Land and Wildlife spoke about the natural beauty of the land. "We would purchase the land and preserve it for habitat, but only if we are sure there are endangered or threatened animals on the property."

"I can assure you there are none," Charles Leon said.

That was Grandpa's cue. He stood up and said in a booming voice, "There *is* endangered wildlife on that land!"

Mr. Leon's smile faded. "Nonsense!"

"Come on, kids." Grandpa herded The Geckos up to the front of the room. "These children have discovered the property is a habitat for endangered wildlife."

I stood at the microphone and took a deep breath.

I told the audience about the screams, the tracks, the claw marks, and the cache with the dead animal.

Mr. Leon interrupted. "Panthers may have traveled through, but that doesn't prove they're living there."

Cassie spoke up. "Then why did you hire someone to capture them and sell them to a private zoo? That's illegal, Mr. Leon."

Charles Leon's face was scarlet. "How *dare* you say such a thing!"

That's when Cassie took out her tape recorder and held it up to the microphone.

CHAPTER 6
Safe Habitat

It was awesome! The audience sat in numb silence as Charles Leon's words burst out over the loud speakers.

We both know there's a family of panthers on this property. You'd better remove them...

"Stop it!" Mr. Leon yelled. "That is not me speaking. I have no idea what this is about."

Then came the hunter's words: *I have someone who wants the animals for his private zoo. He's willing to pay a lot...*

Soon the tape was finished—but Grandpa wasn't.

He held up a blown-up poster of the two men in the woods. It was the clearest, best photo I had ever taken.

"Stop that man!" someone yelled as the hunter, who had been in the audience, tried to sneak out.

Then we Geckos were surprised to see our white-haired friend from the rowboat step up to the microphone.

"It's time I spoke up," he said. "I am Richard Leon, and I am the real owner of this land. You children should be praised for what you've done." He turned to the audience. "My son has tried to convince me that money from the sale of the property would take care of me in my old age. Now I know he was more interested in the money for *himself*."

"Father..." Charles whined, "I was only doing it for you."

Richard Leon glared at his son. "I've decided to preserve the property for wildlife. It will *not* be sold for residential or business use," he announced. He was about to walk away, then turned back to the microphone.

"One more thing," he said. "There are more than just endangered Florida panthers on my property. On that recording I could hear the grasshopper sparrow. It's endangered as well."

The audience clapped and cheered.

The television reporters videotaped the whole thing, and The Geckos made the eleven o'clock news. The headlines the next morning read: *LOCAL KIDS SAVE PANTHERS!*

We learned that Charles Leon and the hunter would have to answer to the authorities for plotting to steal and sell the panthers.

The Geckos were big-time heroes!

Even Mr. Birch was happy with us. He smiled and slapped a hand on Cassie's shoulder.

"Good work, kids," he said with his alligator smile. "All that publicity was great advertising for the park!"

That night, when I finally went to bed, I again heard the shrill scream of the panther. It wasn't a bit scary now.

The thought of our panthers in a protected habitat made me smile. "You're safe now," I whispered as I drifted off to sleep.

Was I dreaming, or did I hear a very loud purr?